Published by
Delacorte Press
Bantam Doubleday Dell Publishing Group, Inc.
666 Fifth Avenue
New York, New York 10103

This edition was first published in Great Britain in 1991 by Andersen Press Ltd.

Library of Congress Cataloging in Publication Data

Shipton, Jonathan.
   Busy! Busy! Busy! / story by Jonathan Shipton; illustrated by Michael Foreman.
       p.   cm.
   Summary: Mother is so busy that she has no time for her child, until, finally, just in time,
she is rescued from her busyness to see a flock of geese.
   ISBN 0-385-30305-X. - ISBN 0-385-30306-8 (lib. bdg.)
   [1. Mother and child - Fiction.]   I. Foreman, Michael, 1938 ill.   II. Title.
PZ7.S5574Bu   1991
[E] - dc20
                                                  90-48518
                                                    CIP
                                                     AC
Manufactured in Italy
October 1991

10   9   8   7   6   5   4   3   2   1

BUSY! BUSY! BUSY!

Story by
JONATHAN SHIPTON
Illustrated by
MICHAEL FOREMAN

Delacorte Press · New York

One fine day
Mom was in a bad mood.
She wouldn't give me a cookie,
or read me a story,
or play,
or anything.

Mom said,
there was too much to do.
She had beds to make and
meals to cook and
clothes to wash.

She said she was chained to the kitchen sink all day!

She said I had to go away and play by myself. So I did!

I went upstairs and sorted out the farm and

I tidied up the cars. I even found a long lost sock.

But all the while down below I could still hear Mom

crashing around with her bad mood. Then suddenly...

the whole house went quiet. I held my breath.

I listened very hard. But I couldn't hear a thing.

So I tip-toed down stairs to see what was going on.

The kitchen door was open a tiny crack. I peeked inside.

There was Mom. Standing very still. Her hands were stuck

in the sink. Two big tears rolled down her cheeks.

In a flash I was onto the chair.

I wiped away her tears.

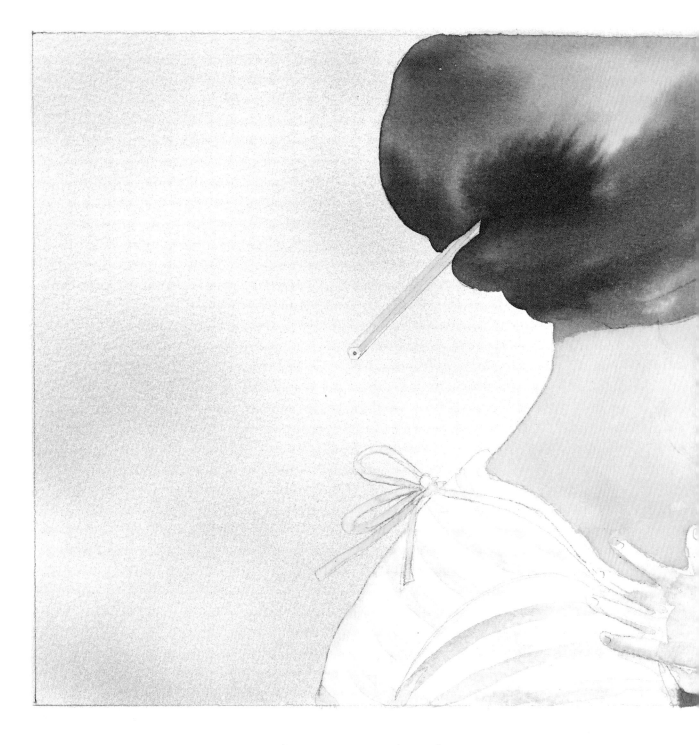

I gave her a great big kiss.

Then I pulled her arms from the water and shouted
"SNIP, SNIP, SNIP!" to the chains around the sink.
They all fell off, like magic.

"Come on Mom," I said, "Quick, before it's too late."
So we grabbed hands and we ran down the hall into
the sunshine.

Just the two of us.

Just in time.